Adapted by Gail Herman

Illustrated by

Carlo Lo Raso and Eric Binder

Scholastic Reader — Level 3

SCHOLASTIC INC.

New York   Toronto   London   Auckland   Sydney
Mexico City   New Delhi   Hong Kong   Buenos Aires

ISBN: 0-439-64151-9

DreamWorks' Shark Tale TM and © 2004 DreamWorks L.L.C.

Published by Scholastic Inc.
SCHOLASTIC, CARTWHEEL BOOKS, and associated logos are trademarks and/or registered trademarks of Scholastic Inc.

12 11 10 9 8 7 6 5 4 3 2 1   4 5 6 7 8/0

Printed in the U.S.A.
First printing, September 2004

It was mealtime. Of course, any time is
mealtime when you're a shark. Lenny's dad,
Don Lino, knew it. Lenny's brother, Frankie,
knew it. Lenny knew it, too. But he didn't
want to eat. Not when the meal was cute
little shrimp.

"Sharks see something, they eat it. That's what sharks do," Lenny's dad told him. Don Lino was the boss of the underwater world. Everyone listened to him.

"Your brother, Frankie, is a real shark. A killer,"
Don Lino told Lenny. "Son, you're going to
learn to be a shark whether you like it or not."

The next day, Lenny went out with Frankie. "This is your last chance to be a real shark," Frankie told Lenny. He pointed to a small fish. "Eat him. Or don't bother coming home!"

The fish was already in trouble. He was tied to a rock. Jellyfish were stinging him—until they spied Lenny. "Shark!" they screamed in fright, then raced away.

Lenny swam up to the fish. He inched closer.
He knew Frankie was watching. Lenny opened
his mouth wide. "I'm not going to eat you,"
Lenny whispered. He whipped his tail around,
acting just like a killer shark.

Then he opened his mouth wide and took a
bite . . . of the rope! The fish was free. "Get
away," Lenny whispered. "Now!"

But Oscar, the tiny fish, didn't understand. He peeked out from behind Lenny. "He's alive!" Frankie cried and shot toward Oscar. Suddenly something fell through the water.
An anchor!

The anchor fell on Frankie. Just like that, Frankie was dead. A terrible feeling came over Lenny. "Noooooo!" he wailed.

Lenny could never be a killer shark. He could never eat fish. What would his father say? He could never go home. Feeling lost and alone, Lenny swam slowly away.

Lenny wandered the ocean, with nowhere to go.

Suddenly, two sharks swam by. "Lennnnnny!" they called.

They're looking for me! Lenny realized. He dove into some nearby weeds. But someone else was hiding there, too. It was that same little fish—Oscar!

Lenny needed to disappear. He needed a plan, and he needed a disguise.

And who better to help him than Oscar? The little fish who was lying to the entire undersea world. *He* was telling everyone that he had killed Frankie. That he was a Sharkslayer. A hero.

But a shark couldn't just hide out in a warehouse. Not when his killer shark dad was looking for him. Lenny needed to lie. To fib.

Lenny gazed around. He loved it—and his new friend, Oscar!

Finally, Lenny persuaded Oscar to hide him in the warehouse at the Whale Wash. It was filled with soaps and sponges and boxes.

"No!" Lenny cried. He grabbed Oscar's tail.
"I don't have anywhere to go," he shrieked.
"Take me with you! You won't even notice
I'm there!"

They kept quiet until the sharks disappeared.
Lenny was in a panic. He'd lost his brother.
He had no home. "Just relax, man," said Oscar.
"Things will work out."

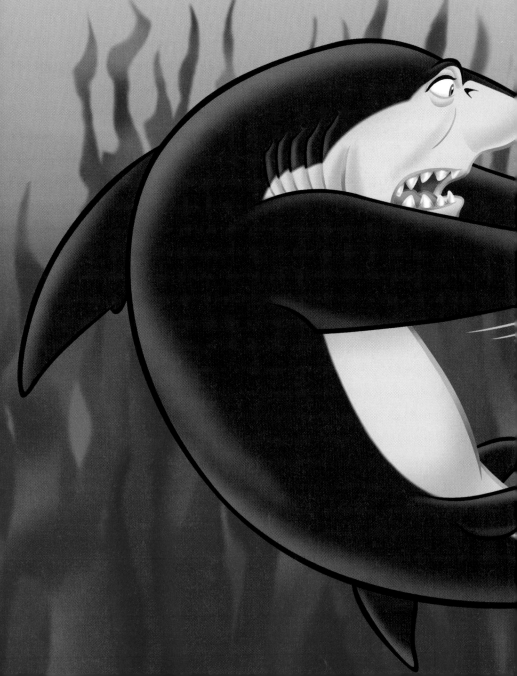

A little later, Lenny jumped out from behind a curtain.

"Tadaaa!" he said. "Sebastian the Whale–Washing Dolphin ready for work!"

Lenny dove into his job at the Whale Wash.
He scrubbed and rubbed and soaped
and rinsed. He liked his job.
He liked his new home.

But it was all a lie . . . dressing as a dolphin and letting his dad think he was a goner like Frankie . . .

Meanwhile, news traveled throughout the reef. Everyone was talking about Oscar the Sharkslayer. Finally, the news reached Don Lino. And that meant trouble. Trouble for Oscar.

Lino came roaring into the Whale Wash. "Swim, Oscar!" Lenny shouted. "Swim for your life!"

Oscar had to do something fast! He raced to
the control booth and pressed a button. Soap
sprayed, lights flashed, and alarms rang. Giant
clamps came down. Oscar wanted to catch
Lino with the clamps, but instead, Lenny was
trapped.

Oscar whirled around. Don Lino was behind him. In a flash, he squeezed through a wall of spinning brushes. Don Lino chased him. But the shark was too big to get through. He was caught—face–to–face with Lenny.

"Lenny?" said Lino. "What are you doing? You're in big trouble!"

"Sorry, Pop," Lenny told him. "But I'll never be a killer shark like you want me to be."

Oscar hugged Lenny. "I love you, man. Just like you are." Then he turned to Don Lino. "Why can't you?"
Don Lino was silent. Then he ordered, "Get me out of here!"
He smiled. "So I can hug my kid!"

"I love you," Don Lino told Lenny. "No matter what."

Lenny sighed happily. No more fishy fibs for him — or Oscar!